Spike,
The Amazing Chicken

A Story From Out West

By George Smith

Gary

Janice

Zach

Gianina

Jon-Macro

Nic

IMPORTANT NOTE: Online Oral Reading Fluency Program Access Code

Visit the URL OR Scan QR code

http://www.lumoslearning.com/a/tedbooks

Access Code: CRSSTC-90371-P

Lumos Learning
Developed by Expert Teachers

Curious Reader Series: Spike, The Amazing Chicken: Includes Online Oral Reading Fluency Practice

ISBN-13: 978-1-949855-14-2

Printed in the United States of America

For permissions and additional information contact:

Lumos Information Services, LLC
Email: support@lumoslearning.com
PO Box 1575, Piscataway,
NJ 08855-1575

Tel: (732) 384-0146
Fax: (866) 283-6471
http://www.LumosLearning.com

Author	-	George Smith
Contributing Author	-	Harini N.
Photo Editor	-	Marco Manfre
Executive Producer	-	Mukunda Krishnaswamy
Designer	-	Sowmya R.

About the Author:

George Smith, a children's book author and publisher, has been conducting writing workshops at schools since 2004. He is passionate about helping young writers turn their creative story ideas to captivating stories that others would enjoy reading. He has authored two children's books, a marine life guide book for science teachers and functioned as an editor for several publications. He lives in Lakewood, New Jersey and loves to travel.

Table of Contents

Introduction

About Spike, The Amazing Chicken

The Story of Spike, The Amazing Chicken is an exciting tale for children in the age group of 7-9. This book is a part of the Lumos Curious Reader series and is designed to help young readers enjoy the story as well and develop their critical reading skills. It includes exercises to create opportunities for young readers to identify settings, plots, characters, etc. The activities are designed to help them recognize how the author has developed the story. This tedBook also includes access to engaging and interactive online resources.

About Curious Reader Series

One of the most enriching experiences for a child is to enjoy stories. The Curious Reader Series by Lumos Learning is designed to provide that special reading experience to help children become successful readers. This series is the perfect package to build students' interest in reading, writing, and language skills.

Each book in the series offers an engaging story that is at a specific reading-level and includes activities that improve reading fluency, reading comprehension, and writing skills. The stories included in the Curious Reader series are fiction by expert children book authors. The activities in the book are tied to tips and pointers that will help children write independently. The stories and activities inspire new ideas and imagination in kids while making reading more enjoyable.

About the Online Fluency Program

Oral reading skills are a critical component of fluency. The students who have developed oral reading fluency, have the ability to read selected passages quickly with few or no errors and show expressions while reading. Research has shown that oral reading fluency is correlated with students' cognitive understanding of the text.

In an industry first, an innovative online fluency improvement program will be accessible to the users of this Lumos tedBook. Parents and educators can easily unlock this access by following the steps provided in the signup section.

The Lumos fluency improvement program is an elearning solution that creates an opportunity for the students to

1. Read, record and listen to the story in their own voice without practice (cold reading)
2. Practice the words included in this story via vocabulary FlashCube and quiz
3. Read-along with an expert story-teller while paying attention to the highlighted text
4. Reread the story, record and listen to the story in their own voice (hot reading)
5. Demonstrate reading comprehension by answering an interactive quiz

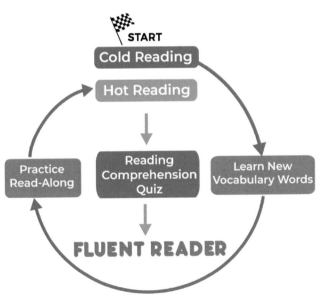

Take Advantage of the Online Oral Fluency Program

To access the online Oral Fluency program included with this book, parents and teachers can register with a FREE account. With each free signup, student accounts can be associated to enable online access for them.

Once the registration is complete, the login credentials for the created account will be sent in an email to the id used during signup. Students can log in to their student accounts to get started with their oral fluency practice. Parents can use the parent portal to keep track of a student's improvement in oral fluency.

How to Register?

Step 1: Go to the **URL** or use the **QR code** for the signup page

> http://www.lumoslearning.com/a/tedbooks

Step 2: Place this book access code
Access Code: CRSSTC-90371-P

Step 3: Fill in the basic details to complete registration

Visit the URL OR Scan QR code

http://www.lumoslearning.com/a/tedbooks
Access Code: CRSSTC-90371-P

To Janice, Gary, Gianina, Nic, Jon-Marco and Zach,
a family who lives in the West
who provided the details about Spike, their chicken
and who assisted with the photography needed to produce this story.

To Spike the chicken, for being so interesting and amazing in her behavior
that she earned her place as the subject of a children's book.

To Dayle Moore, my cousin and mother of Janice,
who told me stories about Spike every time she came back from visiting the family,
thereby planting the seed in my mind
that Spike would make an interesting story for children.

Acknowledgments

The author wishes to acknowledge the administrators, teachers, librarians, media specialists, paraprofessionals, student teachers and students listed below for their assistance in prepublication testing of this book. The feedback they provided was extremely valuable to the author.

ARIZONA: **Aztec Elementary School, Scottsdale:** Dr. Loots, Principal; Mrs. Baldwin, Miss Ely and Mrs. Wilhelm and the students in the Kindergarten and First Grade classes; Miss Hague, Mrs. King, Mrs. Kraatz and Mrs. Laak and the students in the Second and Third Grade classes. **American Heritage Academy, Cottonwood:** Mr. Anderson, Principal; Ms. Grau, Ms. Jessee and Mrs. Allred and the students in their First and Second Grade classes.

NEW JERSEY: **H.C. Johnson Elementary School, Jackson:** Mr. Rosenzweig, Principal; Mrs. Hayden Media Specialist; Miss Van Dusen and her Kindergarten Class; Miss Engel and her First Grade class; Miss Hogan and her Second Grade class; Mrs. Coffey and her Third Grade class; Mrs. Carello and her Fourth Grade class; Mrs. Convery and her Fifth Grade class; **C.W. Goetz Middle School, Jackson:** Mrs. Crate Media Specialist; Mrs. Picchierri and her Seventh Grade class; Mrs. Wapelhorst and her Eighth Grade class. **Memorial Elementary School, Union Beach:** Dr. Franks, Principal; Miss Franey, Special Education Teacher and the Second and Third Grade students at Family Reading Night.

NEW YORK: **P.S. 42 The Eltingville School, Staten Island:** Mrs. LoPresti, Principal; Mrs. Siblo, Library Communication Arts; Miss Francis, Miss G, Mrs. Logan and Mrs. Signorile and their Fourth Grade classes; Miss Garguilo and her Fifth Grade class.

CHAPTER *One*

TV Host: Good morning, kids!

Welcome to The Cowboy George Show, the show from out West that brings you stories about interesting people and animals.

I am Cowboy George, your host. [SP]*

*[SP]: The author recommends that, when reading to a group, you Show the Picture at this point.

Draw the Picture of *Spike* and Color it

Notes

TV Host: We are visiting a ranchette. Do you know what a ranchette is? It's a small ranch — not a lot of land, but enough to raise a small number of animals — and this ranchette has horses, a pig, goats, ponies, dogs, a cat, cockatiels, a rabbit, and chickens.

Come on in, and take a look. [SP]

Search and highlight the below words in the given table.

Cow   Goat   Horse   Pig   Sheep   Hen

S	H	C	S	D	F	H	W	T
H	U	D	G	N	V	O	U	A
E	E	G	E	C	A	R	U	O
E	I	N	N	X	K	S	K	G
P	D	D	T	E	Q	E	Q	H
F	D	W	Y	O	W	E	M	A
Z	N	I	R	C	O	L	A	P
X	M	G	I	V	C	J	U	U
Z	V	H	Y	N	M	Z	R	L

Notes

TV Host: And, speaking of chickens, I would like you to meet Spike, our special guest today. [SP]

As you can see, Spike is a chicken...

Spike: And no ordinary chicken, either.

TV Host: Yes, I mean no, not an ordinary chicken at all. As you will soon find out.

Draw your **favorite** pet animal and color.

Notes

TV Host: This is a picture of the family that lives here...Spike's family... [SP]

Spike: My ADOPTED family! Everyone knows people can't have chickens as children.

TV Host: OK, your adopted family. Here is your other...I mean, your adopted mother... Janice, and our father Gary, and your sister Gianina and brothers Nic, Jon-Marco, and Zach.

Color the Picture of hen and it's family

Notes

Spike: I don't like Zach.

TV Host: Excuse me?

Spike: I don't like Zach. He makes jokes about having me for dinner and...

TV Host: Oh, I'm sure he's kidding. You know how kids like to tease.

Spike: Yes, well I taught him a lesson.

TV Host: How?

Spike: Early one morning, just last month, Janice came out to feed the animals.

When she went back into the house, she forgot to close the back door all the way.

I nudged the door open with my beak, just enough to squeeze through, and went into the kitchen. I don't know where Janice was, but it was very quiet — everyone else was sleeping. Janice had set the table with bowls of cereal. I hopped up on the table, went right to Zach's bowl, and started eating his cereal. [SP]

Notes

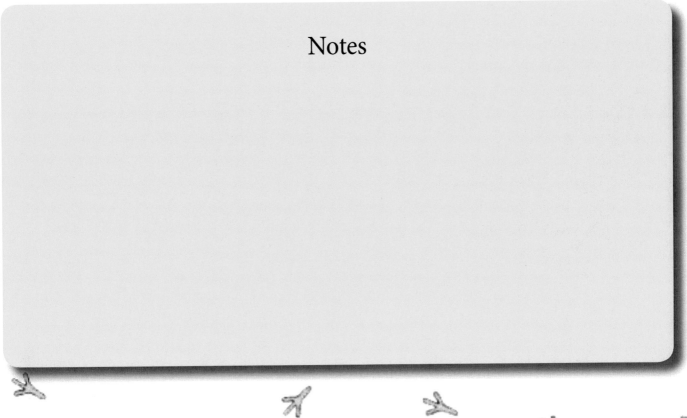

TV Host: Now, wait a minute. How could you tell which bowl was Zach's? Are you psychic or something?

Spike: Well, I...

TV Host: Oh come on!

Spike: OK, his name was on the bowl. So I quickly ate his cereal — it was easy to pick up the chunks. Then I hopped down to the floor and went to the dog's dish. [SP]

One by one, I picked up chunks of dog chow, hopped up onto the table, and placed them in Zach's bowl. I had to make several trips, but finally I transferred all of the chunks. Then I went outside and waited by the back door.

Animals and their young ones

Young one is _____

Young one is _____

Young one is _____

Notes

Spike: Soon all the kids came down for breakfast. Zach looked at his cereal and said, "Hmmm, I guess mom bought a new kind for me to try." So he poured milk on his cereal, took a bite, and made a face. He added some sugar, tried another bite, and smiled. "This is pretty good," he said. The other kids listened, but kept eating. In my mind, I was howling with laughter — it's a good thing chickens can't laugh out loud! [SP]

Complete and color the picture and name the animal

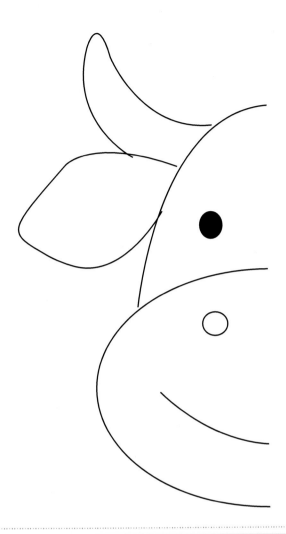

Notes

Spike: Then the dog came in, looked at his empty bowl, and started whining. Gianina said: "I guess mom forgot to feed the dog." So she poured some dog chow in the dog's dish.

Zach watched her pour. "Hey" he said, "that looks like my cereal. It can't be!" He picked up a chunk, looked at it, smelled it, then tasted it. "Arrrgh! It's dog chow! Who did this?"

The other children burst out laughing and started teasing Zach. "Hey Zach, let me hear you bark!" "Hey, Zach, don't wake me up tonight when you howl at the moon!" "Hey, Zach, want me to take you for a walk? I'll get your leash." [SP]

"Verrrry funny," Zach said. "I'll remember this." I was laughing so hard, I had to hold my chest tightly with my wing to keep it from bursting. *(Have me for dinner, will you... you've just been had by a chicken, I thought to myself.)*

Match the animals and their homes

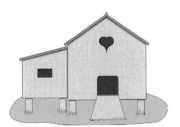

Notes

TV Host: Very funny story, Spike. I can't wait to tell Zach.

Spike: NO, NOOOOH, you can't! PULEEEEZE! I mean you wouldn't do that to a guest on your program, would you?

TV Host: Only kidding, Spike. I won't tell anyone. Viewers, don't go away—we'll be right back with more of Spike, right after this commercial! [SP]

Spike: Wait! Stop! That's a roast chicken in that commercial! How dare you! Get that off the air or I'm walking out of here! That's an insult to all of us chickens! Did Zach make you put that commercial on? That's outrageous!

TV Host: Boys, pull that commercial, NOW! It's ok, Spike. It was on a seven second delay — no one saw it. Sorry.

Spike: You should be! How insensitive! How would you like it if I made a commercial about a roasted TV Host? What is it with these commercials? — chicken, chicken, chicken! Last week my Uncle Henry disappeared. Maybe that was him in the commercial. How about picking on some other animal for a change, like lizards. Yes, a fried lizard sandwich. We have too many lizards out here anyway.

TV Host: Forgive me, Spike. It won't happen again. Let's change the subject.

Notes

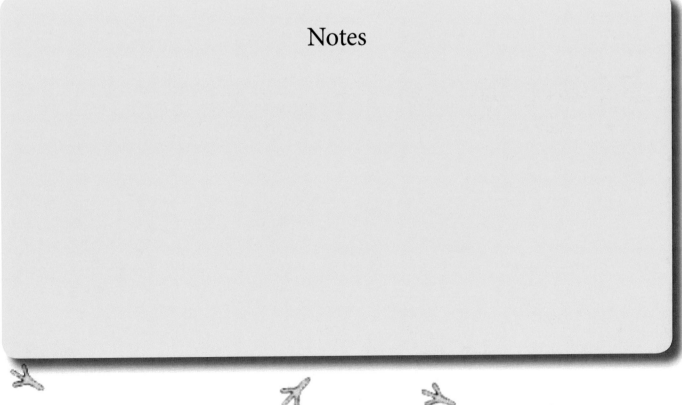

TV Host: Spike, how did you get your name?

Spike: Gianina named me. Look at me — do you see the gold colored feathers mixed in with the black? They look like spikes. That is how I got my name. Cool, huh?

TV Host: Yes Spike, you are one beautiful chicken. (And would look very nice roasting in my oven, thought the TV Host.) [SP]

Complete and color the picture and name the animal

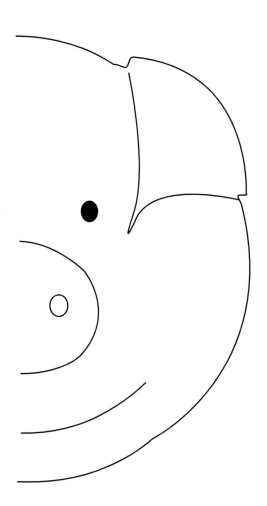

Notes

TV Host: Spike, where do you live on this ranchette?

Spike: Anywhere I want to. (This is a real wise guy, this Spike, thought the TV Host.)

TV Host: Well, exactly where do you consider home?

Spike: The chicken and goat pen over there.

TV Host: Where the other chickens are?

Spike: Of course. Haven't you ever heard the expression "Birds of a feather flock together"?

TV Host: I take it you don't always stay in the chicken pen.

Spike: I have the run of this ranchette — I go wherever I want.

TV Host: But I see a fence and a gate. How do you get out?

Spike: It's magic. I close my eyes, flap my wings three times, mutter abracadabra, and...

TV Host: Oh come on, Spike!

Spike: Okay. This is how I do it. See the wire fence? I hop up on the fence and scrunch my body to make it narrower. Then I squeeze through the fence and land on the ground on the other side. [SP]

Notes

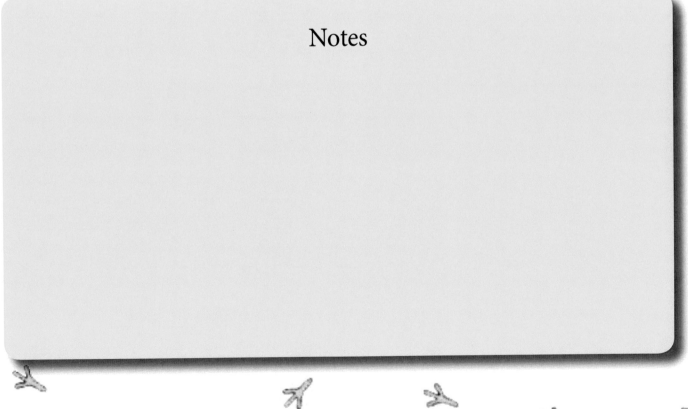

TV Host: Very clever. Once you get out, what do you do?

Spike: I look for TV Hosts to interview me.

TV Host: You're kidding!

Spike: Duuuuh.

TV Host: Duuuuh? That's a word humans use.

Spike: Not anymore. Actually, there is something very important that I do before I get out. I'm the first animal to wake up, and the very first thing I do is wake up all the other animals. I don't believe in sleeping late — there is too much to do, too much fun to have, too much life to live! Besides... I'm hungry. So I hop up on the roof of the goat house and I wake them all up.

TV Host: How?

Spike: Like this: Cock-a-doodle-do!

TV Host: But that's the sound a rooster makes, and you are a hen, not a rooster.

Spike: Took me years of practice to get that right. Since we don't have a rooster, I'm it!

TV Host: Does it work?

Spike: Yes, it works. As you can see in this picture, all of the animals are awake... [SP]

...except...

Notes

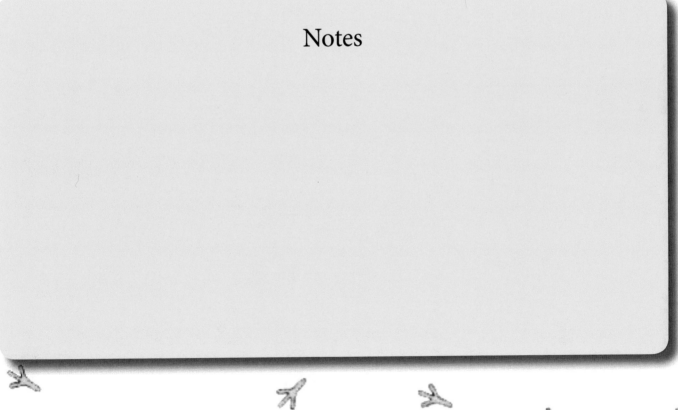

Spike: Hammy the pig. [SP]

You know how pigs are — they like to sleep late, so sometimes I have to go over and peck on his tummy. When he wakes up, of course I run away.

TV Host: Why do you run?

Spike: Why do I run? There's 200 pounds of angry pig chasing me! Helloooo! But he gets over it as soon as his breakfast arrives. Anyway, they all wake up hungry.

Color the Picture of Hammy, the pig.

Notes

Spike: But, there was a problem — the kids were not coming out to feed us right away. We had to wait, sometimes for a long time. But then we figured out a way to hustle them along.

TV Host: And how do you animals hustle kids along? I have kids; I've tried everything, and I can't get them to move quickly at all in the morning.

Spike: All the animals got together and started calling them. Yesirree, can you imagine the noise that we made? Cock-a-doo-dle-do, cluck cluck, oink oink, neigh-a-a-a-a, bleat bleat, and woof woof, all at once? What a racket! It was enough to wake up the entire neighborhood! And the first few times we did it, it DID wake up the entire neighborhood! [SP] The neighbors must have called and complained, because, from that day on, just a few minutes after my Cock-a-doodle-do in the morning, one of the kids always comes out to feed THEM.

Match the animal to it's sound by drawing arrows

woof woof

oink oink

neigh-a-a

cluck cluck

bleat bleat

Notes

TV Host: Feed THEM? You mean "Feed US."

Spike: No, I mean feed THEM. Do you think a chicken with my talents would be satisfied with plain chicken feed?

TV Host: Well yes, I...

Spike: So, you think I'm a dumb cluck? That's it — this interview is over!

TV Host: Quick boys, run a commercial. Wait, Spike! Please don't go. I apologize.

Spike: First you run a commercial with a roast chicken, and then you insult me!

TV Host: Please don't leave!

Spike: If you will cluck for me, I'll stay.

TV Host: We're on television — I'm a big star — I can't do that...! Why are you glaring at me? Ok... CLUCK!! Are you happy now?

Spike: Yes — you can get off your knees. [SP]

TV Host: How did it happen that you don't eat chicken feed?

Notes

Spike: One day, I followed Jon-Marco to the back door. I watched the kids eating breakfast and, guess what? They don't eat chicken feed. I needed to try their food...but how? Ahhh, yes. Here's how. I stood outside the back door, clucking continuously and staring at them while they were eating breakfast. [SP1-cover SP2]

I repeated this for two more days. I knew they saw me, although they pretended they didn't. Well, on the fourth day, they had had enough. Gianina — she's the smart one in the bunch — guessed that I wanted some food, so she prepared a bowl of lettuce and bread and placed it on the ground. [SP2] It tasted great! Much better than chicken feed!

So now, every day, I go to the back door and someone brings me cereal or bread and lettuce or potato peelings or salad greens or dog or cat food or chocolates.

TV Host: Chocolates?

Spike: Not really — just wanted to see if you were listening. One day, they brought a boiled egg. Cluck — I mean — Yuk! It was awful! They saw me turn up my nose — I mean my beak — at the egg and they never brought an egg again. I guess they thought, if I laid the egg, I would enjoy eating it. Rawwwwng!

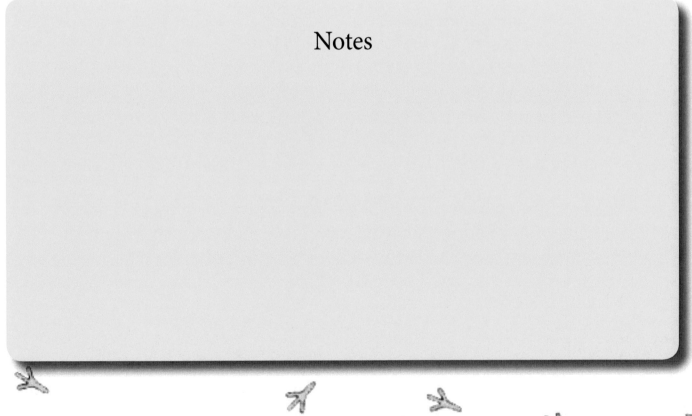

Notes

TV Host: Tell me more.

Spike: I think it's my duty to look out for the other animals — you know, make sure they are all right, not stressed out or anything.

TV Host: I see — should I call you Dr. Chicken?

Spike: Call me Dr. Spike. Open wide, and say, "Ahhh!" I SAID...

TV Host: I heard you, and I am NOT going to open wide! We're on television — I'm a big star — I can't do that! What kind of stress do you mean?

Spike: Like being in labor.

TV Host: You mean giving birth?

Spike: Duuuuh. Just last month, Nanny — she's a goat — went into labor. She was bleating pitifully — she was in pain — and she continued for a long time. I was worried. It was hot out there, and the family was staying in the house. I had to get their attention!

I squeezed through the fence, ran halfway to the house, and stood there squawking as loudly as I could. I squawked and squawked until Janice came out to see what the problem was. I walked toward the goat pen, continuing to squawk, so she would follow me. [SP]

When she reached the goat pen, she saw Nanny and realized that the goat needed help delivering her baby, and. a few minutes later, she helped Nanny deliver a healthy baby goat.

TV Host: Oh, a goatee.

Spike: Very funny.

Notes

TV Host: You're a hero!

Spike: No. I'm a chick...oh, I see what you mean. Hmmm... that explains why Janice picked me up, hugged me, stroked my feathers, and carried me to the kitchen where she gave me a special treat. [SP]

TV Host: Well, kids, we have run out of time for today. Tune in tomorrow for the rest of our interview with Spike, the amazing chicken and her family. Bye.

--- End of CHAPTER ONE ---

Match the animals and their homes

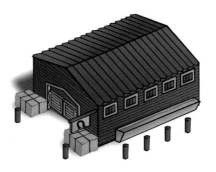

Notes

TV Host: Good morning, kids! This is Cowboy George, your host, welcoming you once again to The Cowboy George Show. Today we are continuing our visit to the ranchette where an amazing chicken named Spike lives. Oh, look — who is this coming toward us?

Spike: It's Jon-Marco. [SP]

TV Host: Hi, Jon-Marco. Come on over. Would you be willing to answer some questions?

Jon-Marco: Sure. I always wanted to be on TV. What do you want to know?

TV Host: Tell us some things about Spike.

Animals and their young ones

Young one is   _____

Young one is   _____

Young one is   _____

Notes

41

Jon-Marco: Almost every day, after breakfast, Spike visits the horses. On really hot days, she drinks from their water tub and stands in their shadows, where it is cooler. On rainy days, she stands under them to keep dry. Sometimes she eats their feed, but they don't seem to mind. [SP1-cover SP2]

Next, she visits the pig. Then she returns to her pen to visit the goats. And if her favorite goat looks like she is ready to take her nap, Spike takes her nap too...on the goat.

TV Host: On the goat?

Spike: Yes, on the goat...you don't believe me, do you? Look at this picture. [SP2] See? I am standing on her back and, in a minute, I will squat and begin my nap.

TV Host: How can you sleep on the back of a goat? Won't you fall off?

Spike: No. The goat isn't moving — she is taking her nap too, and I gently wrap a few of her long coat hairs around my claws. Then I take my nap. You may be a big TV star, but you'll never have the pleasure of sleeping on a goat!

TV Host: Mercy me! How will I ever get over that?

Notes

TV Host: Jon-Marco, are there more funny stories about Spike?

Jon-Marco: Yes. Another day, I came home and walked into the living room. Spike was sleeping on the horse. I couldn't believe my eyes...

TV Host: Hold it! I can't believe my EARS. There was a horse in your living room? A horse?

Jon-Marco: Yes. What's so unusual about that? This IS the West, and we do love our horses, you know.

TV Host: Yes, but a horse in the living room? What a mess — your house must smell like a barn!

Jon-Marco: Oh, it's not a real horse; it's a statue. And perched in the saddle, was Spike, fast asleep. Here — look at this picture. [SP] Are you with me now?

TV Host: Phew!! You had me worried for a moment, but now I understand. I should have realized that this happens all the time in our country. I'm sure most of our viewers have at least one horse in their living rooms with a sleeping chicken in the saddle and...

Spike: Get real with your humor. I walked into the house that day to see more TV, but the TV set was off. The house was quiet, and suddenly, I felt very tired — too tired to walk all the way outside for my usual goat nap. Besides, I always wondered what it would feel like to sit on a saddle. So I hopped up on the arm of the couch, from there to a shelf, and then onto the rear end of the horse. I walked to the saddle and sat in it. It was VERRRY comfortable, and soon I fell asleep. Could they let me enjoy my nap? Nooooo! I heard a noise, opened my eyes, and there was Jon-Marco taking pictures.

TV Host: Well, you do make a handsome cowboy, or whatever you call something with a beak and feathers sitting on a horse.

(I agree with Zach — she would look better on a barbecue grill, thought the host.)

Notes

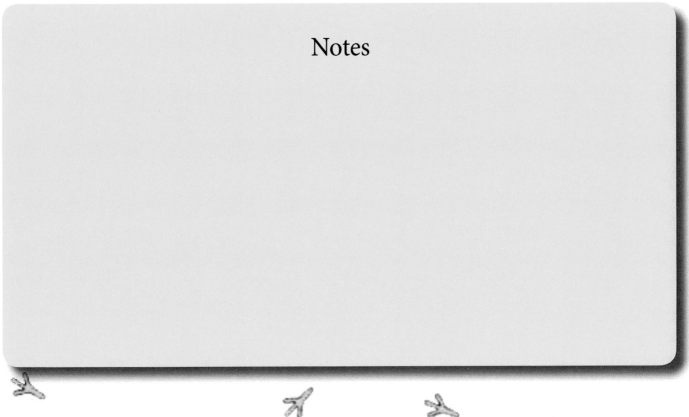

Jon-Marco: I have another one for you. One day, I saw Spike talking to a teddy bear.

Imagine — Spike thinking a teddy bear was real!

Spike: What!! I did not.

Jon-Marco: Did too.

Spike: Did not.

Jon-Marco: Here's the picture. [SP]

Spike: I knew it wasn't real.

Jon-Marco: Did not.

Spike: Did too.

TV Host: Staaaaahp, you two, now! That's enough. Thank you for stopping by, Jon-Marco. We enjoyed your stories.

Jon-Marco: You're welcome. Let me know if you need a host to interview rock stars or TV personalities — I'm available. Bye.

Notes

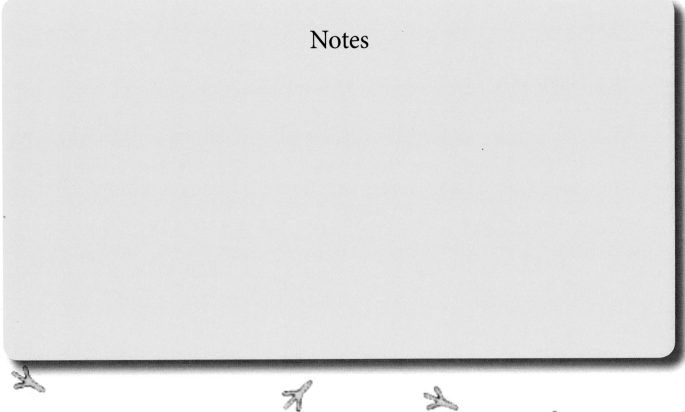

TV Host: Spike, what else do you do?

Spike: Lay eggs.

TV Host: Lay eggs?

Spike: Lay turquoise eggs.

TV Host: Lay turquoise eggs?

Spike: Is there an echo in here? Yes, I lay turquoise eggs.

TV Host: Aren't chicken eggs usually brown or white?

Spike: Theirs are.

TV Host: Whose are?

Spike: My pen mates.

TV Host: Why aren't yours?

Spike: I am a CLASSIER chicken. Look at me: I have gold colored feathers among the black, and I can crow like a rooster. So why should I lay ordinary eggs? Look at these. [SP]

Notes

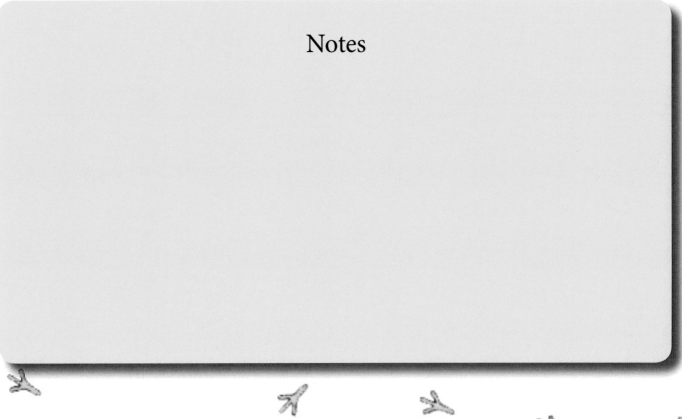

TV Host: I'm convinced that you're not an ordinary chicken, but I'll bet even YOU aren't perfect. You must have gotten in trouble for doing something wrong sometime in your life.

Spike: Not me. I'm perfect.

TV Host: Aw, come on, Spike.

Spike: OK, I'm not perfect. The cat got mad at me once. The family left on vacation and the person who came to feed us didn't realize that I didn't eat chicken feed. I was hungry and didn't know what to do, so I walked around to the front porch and smelled something really good. It came from the cat's dish. I ate most of it. [SP]

TV Host: Where was the cat?

Spike: Who knew? Who cared? He wasn't there. Finders Keepers.

TV Host: How did he find out that you ate his food?

Spike: I made a mistake — I tripped and lost my balance, and accidentally stepped in the cat's dish and left a claw mark in the food. No other animal leaves a claw mark like a chicken, so he figured it out.

TV Host: What did he do about it?

Spike: Hung out by his dish each day, waiting for his food, and then ate it right away.

Notes

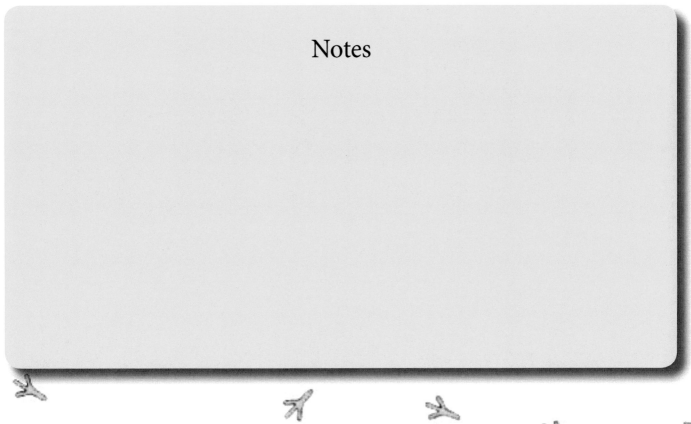

Spike: Which reminds me...I got in trouble for some other some claw prints.

TV Host: Really.

Spike: One day, I walked around to the front porch and there was a tile man spreading this gray gooey stuff and carefully placing some tiles in it. I had never seen this before, so I came closer to watch. When he saw me, he waved his arms and yelled to shoo me away. It worked...or so he thought. He should have realized with WHOM he was dealing!

Anyway I came back after he left, walked across the porch on the tiles, and then I stepped in the gray stuff. My foot sank in; it felt cool, and when I removed my foot, guess what? There was a perfect claw mark, a true work of art, so I made some more claw prints. They will stay there forever as proof that Spike was there. [SP]

Search and highlight the below words in the given table.

Chicken   Cattle   Dog   Buffalo   Goat   Bull   Duck

F	C	K	J	H	Y	G	B	R
Q	H	M	N	I	K	C	U	D
W	I	P	I	N	M	C	F	O
E	C	O	M	O	A	G	F	K
R	K	B	U	T	L	P	A	V
T	E	U	T	Z	V	G	L	G
B	N	L	S	I	S	D	O	G
U	E	L	S	C	B	A	O	M
I	X	C	B	Z	T	B	R	I

Notes

Spike: The next day, Gary came to my pen. He glared at me, grabbed me, and carried me to the front porch. He held my head down close to the claw prints, so I could see them. Then he stood and pointed his finger at my face, and said in a loud voice, "Bad chicken! Bad chicken! Bad chicken!" The kids heard this and came running to the front door; and when they figured out what I had done, they started laughing hysterically and yelling "Bad chicken!" [SP]

Then Gary realized how funny he looked yelling at a chicken and he started laughing too, and let me go. But, I'll tell you — if I had the chance, I would do it again!

Look at the empty farm and draw the animals that live on the farm and color.

Notes

TV Host: Very entertaining. Well, it seems that you have told us about each member of your adopted family except for Nic. Anything you want to tell us about Nic?

Spike: Oh yes, Nic...I like Nic best of all. He always handles me gently. He has an egg business, you know — I think he supports the whole family — and every day, he comes to collect our eggs, and everyday, I have one for him. Oh, look — there he goes now to make his deliveries. [SP]

He makes a big fuss over my eggs because they are turquoise. I heard him tell Janice that mine are more valuable.

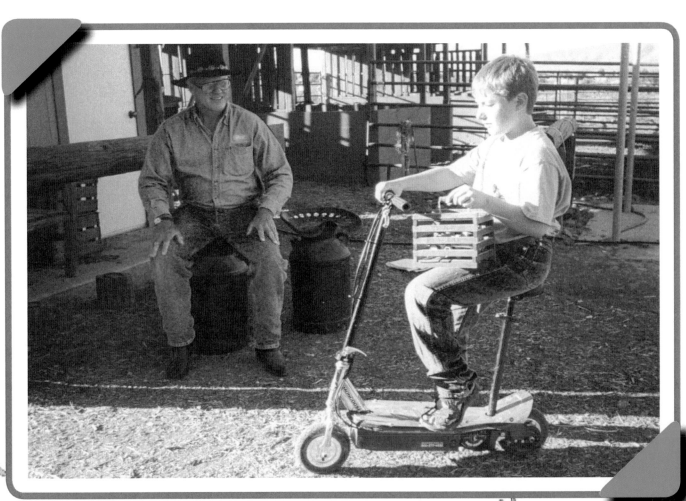

Circle the animals which are part of the story.

Notes

Spike: And one more thing — the best of all. Nic is the only one who knows how to put me to sleep. I love it.

TV Host: How do you put a chicken to sleep? Hmmm...let me guess. You put on soft music, feed it milk and cookies, and sing to it.

Spike: Your humor is so corny you should be on televis...oops, you already are.

Anyway, he tucks my head gently under my wing, folds the wing over my head, and gently rocks me back and forth, and, before you know it, I am feeling drowsy, and then I fall asleep. It's awesome! [SP]

Help Spike, find the way to reach Nic

Notes

TV Host: Well Spike, this has been one of the best interviews I have ever conducted on The Cowboy George Show. Thank you for allowing me to interview you, and I wish you the best of cluck — er — luck.

Spike: Thank you too. I enjoyed it, except for the chicken commercial.

TV Host: Be sure to tune in next week at this time when we will interview a little red boat about its journey down a Maine river.* This is Cowboy George signing off. [SP]

* This is a reference to Mr. Smith's first book, ***The Journey of the Little Red Boat*** *A Story from the Coast of Maine*, for children six to eight years old.

--- The End ---

Color the below picture

Notes

Listen to the Story and Practice Read-Along on StepUp App

Step 1

Scan this QR code 1 to download StepUp App

Step 2

Open 'Scan and Learn' in the StepUp App and scan below QR code.

Listen to the audio version of "Spike, The Amazing Chicken" story and practice Read-Along.

Readability and Related Details

Rating	A
Category	Fiction
Words	4149
Unique words	904
Sentences	456
Reading Time	18-26 minutes
Age Group	7 - 9 yrs

The Use of Nonfiction, Realistic Fiction, and Fantasy in This Story

Nonfiction:
1. The ranchette, the family that lives there, Spike the chicken and the other animals in the story are real.
2. Spike comes into the house occasionally, on her own, when the back door is left open.
3. Spike and the other chickens share a pen with the goats. Spike squeezes through the fence nearly every day, and visits the horse corral, where she eats horse feed, drinks from the trough, stands in the horses' shadows on very hot days or stands under the horses when it rains. She also visits the pig.
4. Spike can crow like a rooster.
5. All the animals make noise in unison only when they see Janice peering out the back door at them early in the morning, to let her know they are hungry.
6. Spike eats human food, cat and dog food (which she steals from their bowls), and horse feed. Spike stood outside the back door clucking continuously and watching the family eating breakfast until someone brought her some food. This started a routine that occurs every day.
7. When a goat was having difficulty giving birth, Spike squawked loudly for a long time until Janice came out of the house and walked to the goat pen, where she helped the goat give birth.
8. Spike takes her naps on the back of one of the goats.
9. Spike stood and watched the television screen for a long time one day.
10. Cockatiels can chirp, whistle and imitate other sounds, such as a dog barking.
11. Spike climbed into the saddle of the horse statue in the living room and took a nap. To do this, she hopped from the floor to the couch, then hopped up on the arm of the couch, then jumped up on the shelf nearby, then jumped onto the hindquarters of the horse and walked forward to the saddle.
12. Spike spent several minutes talking to a teddy bear one of the kids left on the floor in the house.
13. Spike lays turquoise eggs and makes a big fuss over each one.
14. Spike left her claw prints in the fresh cement on the front porch.

Realistic Fiction:
1. The Cowboy George Show is not real, and any relationship to an actual show by that name is purely coincidental.
2. The family never used the technique for putting a chicken to sleep; that technique has been used by a friend of mine, Keith Sayre, from Missouri.
3. No one remembers what was on TV when Spike was watching it.
4. Gary carrying Spike to the front porch and scolding her for leaving footprints is fictitious. In reality, the family thought the incident was funny and left the claw prints in the cement.

Fantasy:
1. Spike being interviewed by a TV Host, and conversing in English.
2. Spike eating Zach's cereal and transferring dog chow into his bowl.
3. Spike getting angry when seeing the roast chicken commercial and the cockatiels on TV.
4. Spike pecking on the pig's stomach to wake him up, then running away.

Reading Proficiency Progress Chart

Name	Time Spent	Teacher Score	Actual Words	Student Words	Words Correct	Words Wrong	Words Missing	Text Score	Audio Score

Made in the USA
Columbia, SC
17 September 2020